Shhhh . . . Don't Tell!

Robyn A. Banks-Harris

AuthorHouse™
1663 Liberty Drive
Bloomington, IN 47403
www.authorhouse.com
Phone: 1 (800) 839-8640

Published by AuthorHouse 09/13/2018

ISBN: 978-1-5462-5795-0 (sc)
978-1-5462-5796-7 (e)

Print information available on the last page.

This book is printed on acid-free paper.

authorHOUSE®

First of all, I would like to dedicate this book to all the children, who experience domestic violence either first hand or indirectly

I would also like to dedicate it to New Direction of Hope, LLC and Frontline Service, where I received most of my education and training

To my daughter's Brittany Banks and Yasmine Saleem who along with my grandchildren (The Snuggle Bunch Kids) modeled my story.

And my other number one supporters: Timothy Harris, Ruth Banks (my mom), Walter Banks (My dad), and Alicia Mallory (My niece) who all took time out to repeatedly listen to my story and give me honest feedback.

Hey you wanna hear a secret

What I heard the other day

I heard daddy hitting mommy

Thought I was out to play

FUN
IN
THE

He said that she was worthless

She could never do things right

As he yelled so many things to her

I shut my eyes real tight

That's when I heard her crying

Couldn't take it anymore

I planned to go protect her

When I busted through the door

436

You know I felt so helpless

There was nothing I could do

And that's why I called you here today

To share my secret thoughts with you

Daddy looked at me surprised

And mommy held me back

Then he threw the remote at me

And now my eye is turning black

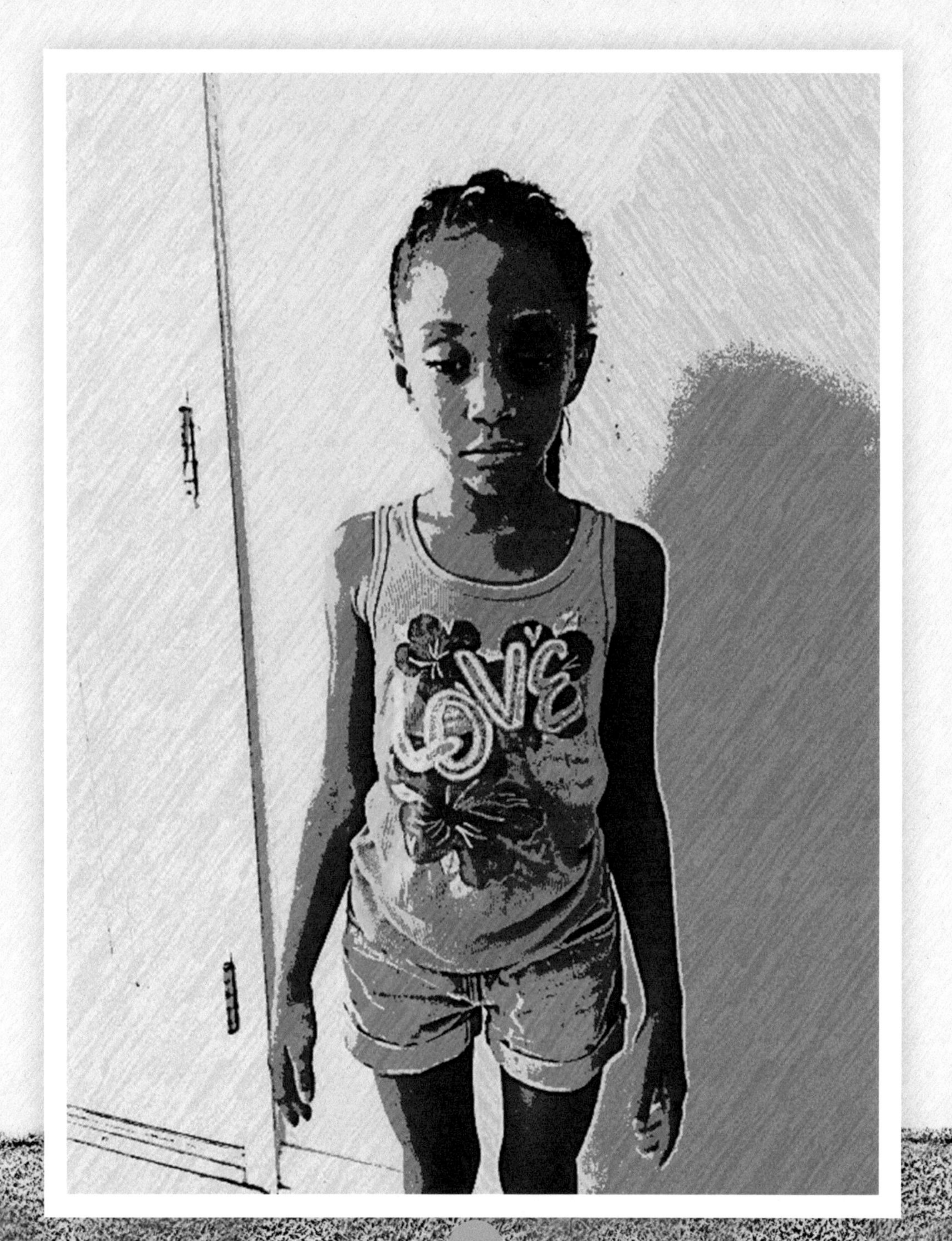
LOVE

You must promise, don't tell anyone

Must be something that I did

I will clean the house from up to down

They'll be glad I am their kid

Oh you know I love you Toot

I just want this mess to end

You will always be my buddy

You're my very special friend

But I'll just talk to Nana

She can help you work through this

I will let her know what's going on

With Mr. and the Mrs.

I barely got to sleep that night

The pain was in my head

A monster tried to get me

But the monster was my dad

He said I have a treat for you

You'd better come real quick

But as soon as I could grab it

He beat me with a stick

And now I'm up and sweating

Have no one that I can call

Cause I cannot wake my daddy

Or there's trouble for us all

And plus I need dry clothing

For this crazy mess I did

Last night I wet my covers

In the garbage can I hid

Mommy called me down to breakfast

I must hurry on to school

But I didn't want to go today

Cause kids can be so cruel

I was always taught a lesson

To never tell a lie

But they'll want to hear the story

Of what happened to my eye

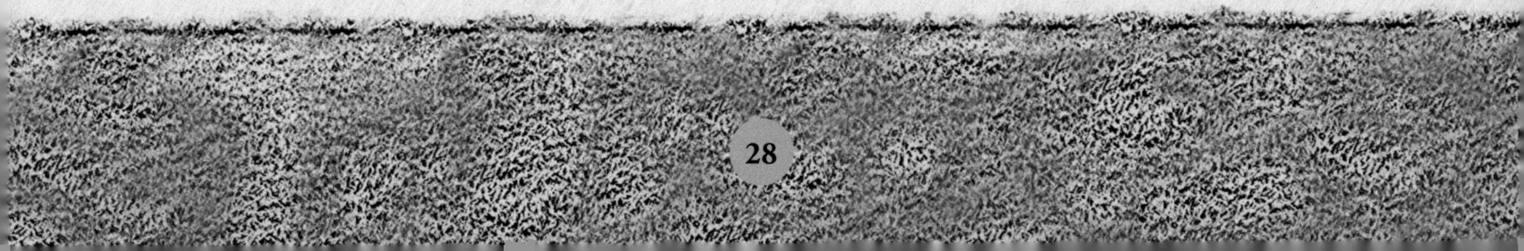

Now mommy's all upset with me

For not eating all my food

Said that other kids are starving

I am stubborn and so rude

I cannot eat, I cannot sleep

She wouldn't understand

Don't want to talk to anyone

Not even to my friends

When daddy walked into the room

Mommy jumped up and said

Here's your book bag, lunch and sneakers

Now go on to school she said

Weeks went the same inside my house

The matches, screams and shouts

I put my shiny headphones on

To drown the noises out

At school I felt so tired

But what more could I do

I saw my best friend down the hall

Dee can I talk to you

KIND
HEAR
FIERCE
MIND
BRAVE
SO

Dee hugged and reassured me

That everything would be okay

She said her Nana had made plans

To come to school today

I'm so scared I'll get in trouble

For telling them about

All the arguments and fighting

That goes on inside my house

What if they come and take me

Out my house cause I've been bad

Cause I didn't clean the table

Or the dishes that I had

BELiEVE
in your dreams

Dee's Nana, mom and teacher

Took me in the room to talk

Started off the conversation

Saying: "This is not your fault"

There's many other children

Going through the same thing too

That's why we're sitting here today

To give support to you

I admire your strength and courage

Seeking help from us today

You have taken the first step

Of bringing change about your way

And I know that this is hard for you

That's why we're gonna be

Here to help you through this crisis

And to help your family

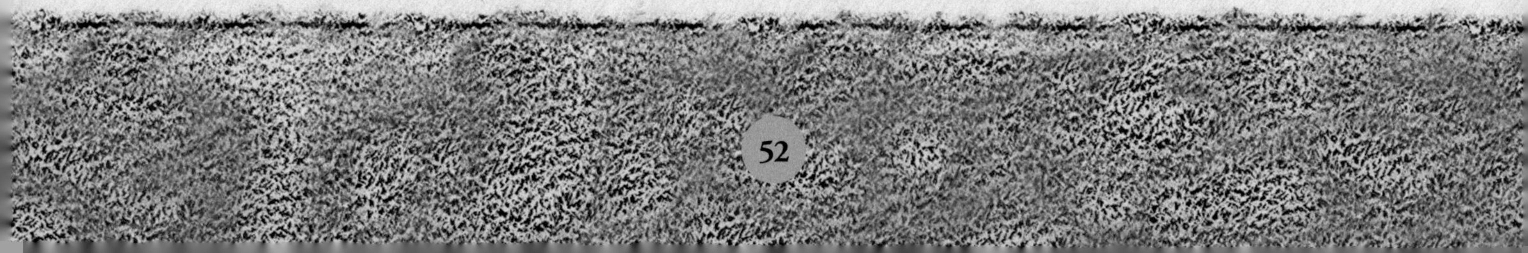

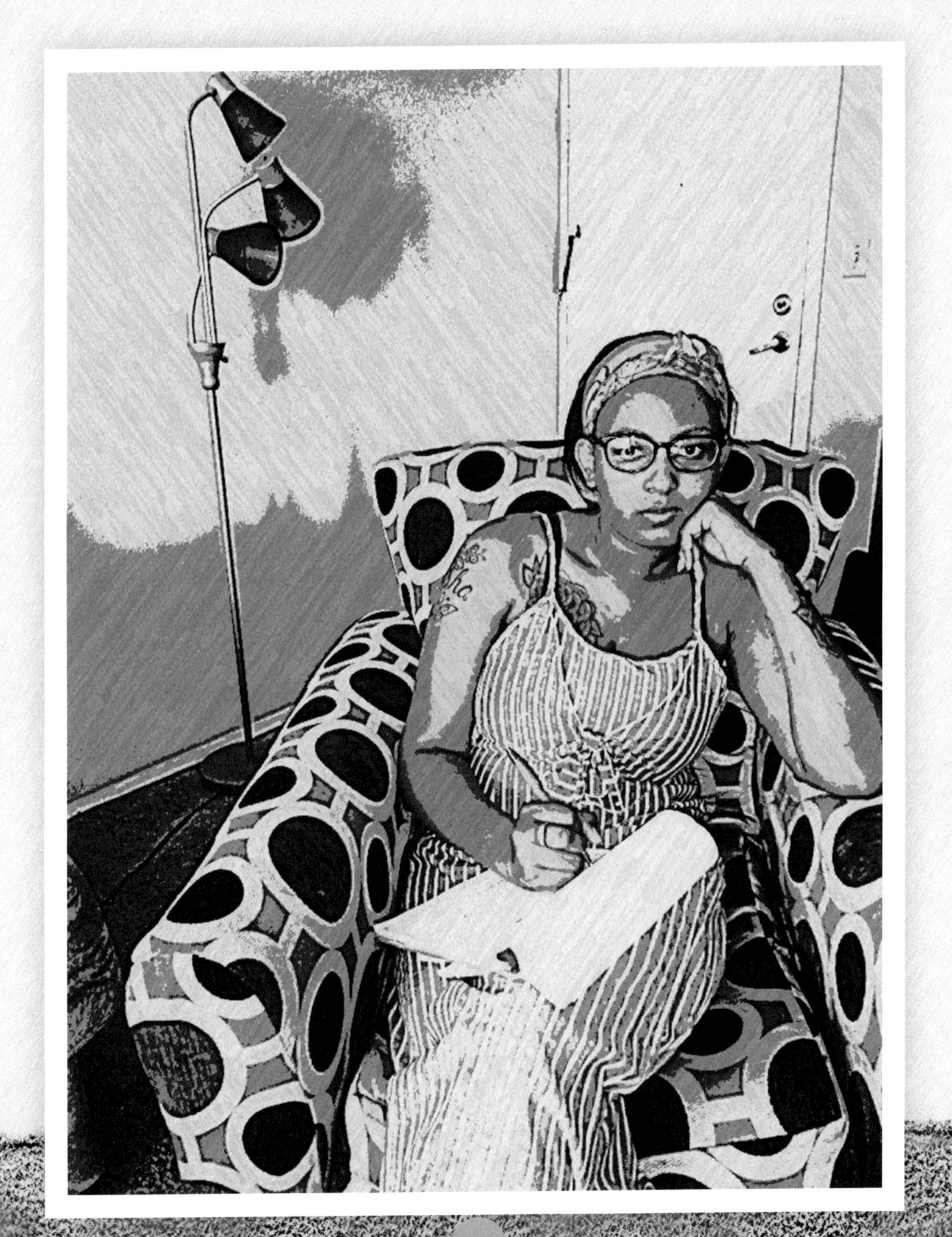

Thanks Ms. Nana and the rest of you

For being by my side

Now I may live more peacefully

No more monsters or tears I hide

Nana's Lesson

Domestic violence affects many children worldwide. And in order to bring about change, you must tell someone, even if it is a friend that you trust. There are agencies that could help you and provide support and encouragement. And just remember...I LOVE YOU ♥

CHARACTER PAGE

Nana

Ms. Shelley

Ms. Nicky

Robyn

Brittany

Yasmine

Toot

Dee

Princess

Jayde

Jordynn

Karsyn

Angel

Pooh

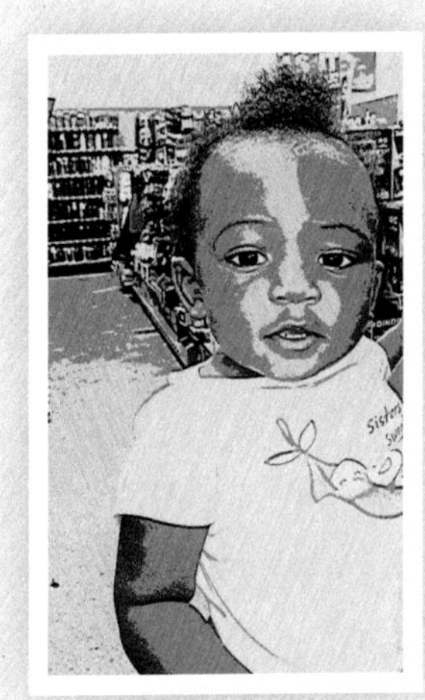

Mari

Jayla

Kaelyn

Kha’mari

Reviews

Shhhh! Don't Tell! Is a must read for every adult that interacts with children-from volunteers to professionals. The book speaks honestly from the viewpoint of a child enabling adults to gain insight into the silent suffering of youth living with this form of toxic stress. It will also serve as ready resource to assist young people in gaining the confidence to speak about their emotions and fears.

Kenya Fike MBA
Grants Manager

Shhhh Don't Tell, by Robyn Harris is an easy to read book written from the perspective of the child witnessing g domestic violence in her own home. This book is a great tool for a professional or concerned person who knows a child struggling with the issues associated with domestic violence. The author offers a careful and sensitive look at the behaviors associated with the emotional and social and cognitive aspects of witnessing domestic violence.

Laura Camp
MSSA, LSW

Printed in the United States
By Bookmasters